floating

a short story

Pianta

"Words are a pretext. It is the inner bond
that draws one person to another, not words."

Rumi

Preface

If we lose the bond that Rumi speaks of, will we lose our desire for words? If we regain that bond, will we desire words again?

floating

A thin, bird-like man sat on a bench, his arms straining across the bulging suitcase that lay on his lap. No one had noticed when he had walked from the roadside to the water, struggling with the case packed beyond capacity.

It had become commonplace to see people hauling bags, suitcases, duffels, carts, wagons to unload what they had into the blue water—water that was filled with sea creatures and many, many thoughts: thoughts captured in the shape of words. Some thoughts were whole, some were partial, and others lived as fragments, while still others slid through miles of unconscious streams.

People read, wrote, and spoke, but they were now disinterested in words and shaping thoughts into words. They found arranging and rearranging them tiresome, and they began to toss them out wherever they could.

The water was unprepared to fend for itself. People dumped their thoughts into it, and like the uneasy man on the bench who eventually tossed all that he had in that case and left, they cast their expressions adrift. What they dumped was a stray letter here or there ... a word or phrase ... sometimes a punctuation mark, which, like driftwood, would knock itself against the rocks, wearing itself down. Bits of an alphabet letter or phrases would pop up in strange places, and people would rummage through them, leaving the majority behind like trash.

On a day that the waters were particularly cramped, a water creature told herself, "This has got to stop. These words and marks need a place to go." She swam along the shore and started looking for people, but she saw no one. She thought, "People are gone. They don't use words. They don't have use for them at all." On that day she held letters to her chest and swam as if to give them comfort. She tried to untangle strings of sentences that were trapped around sea grass and coral beds, even though she didn't know how one ended and the other began. She would coo to them, thinking they might appreciate that.

Then on a day close to winter, she sensed someone was near. Not to frighten anyone, she kept below but followed the shadow of someone walking very near the water. "Who is it?" she wondered. "What is it?" she wondered. Then the shadow drew away and the air felt lonely and empty again.

The next morning she swam near the shore again, but the emerald of her fins, the goldfish-like train of her tail, the light falling upon her was so lovely that she became lost in that moment. She wanted to feel the sun in those cold spots and how the water moved through in her hair and over her arms. She spent hours in a gentle float until she remembered her goal. "Drowsy and dull," she realized, as the letter "D" drifted by, and she remembered her intentions and lifted herself up out of the water to see if anyone was on shore.

Luckily, Mr. M had just turned away at that moment, for the sight of the creature would have frightened him. As he looked away, the mermaid thought quickly and tossed a "W" and a punctuation mark at his feet and dove back into the water. "That," she said, "is doing my part," and she swam away, never to think of him again.

For Mr. M, this was an odd moment. He had not come to the ocean for many, many years. It was too cold, too far, and he preferred to stay in his cottage and feel the silence in the walls. He didn't know what exactly had happened, but he would soon find out.

With the slap of water and the splat of sand, Mr. M saw the stray "W," which he mistook at first as an "M," and an accompanying exclamation mark lying near his feet. *What*, he thought. He hammered his knuckle on the tin letter. He looked around and saw the driftwood of old sentences and worn out letters splitting themselves on the rocks. These ruined things were spewing out from the ocean.

Unusual things did not happen to Mr. M; he led an unremarkable life. However, his comportment was that of a notable man. He dressed simply but chose good wool and garments that suited his solid frame. His wife had fallen for him rather quickly, for his initial impression hadn't been lost on her. He appeared as a portly Peter Sellers, who was popular in films at the time. Like Sellers, he had dark hair and a mustache, and too, a serious air, which could go several ways. People were unsure of him. His casual remarks seemed to hover between genuine seriousness or borderline pretension.

Odd, he thought, as he stooped over to examine what lay at his feet. There was something that interested him, so even though it was slightly uncomfortable to lean over to examine the letters further, he did. He sniffed them. Sea salt, he thought. *Worn but still useful*, he thought. With sun warming him, he picked up several stray pieces even though they were an inconvenience, and he popped them into his carrying sack. "Hurry home," he said, to no one in particular.

That night he said a few words to his wife, slid the pieces in the closet where he hung his coat, and went to sleep.

In the morning, he had his coffee and read his morning paper. His wife was at the market—she was careful about produce—and wouldn't be home for hours. Their lives were based on simple routines designed by choice, and their choices gave each other room and ease.

Feel no pressure, he thought, feeling exactly that when he thought of inspecting his treasures. He pulled them out and looked at them. He set them first on the table, turning each letter carefully to judge its condition. He placed a letter, then a punctuation mark, and so on, till all seven pieces sat in front of him.

The wooden pieces were flat and grayish, and those that were metal were pitted and uneven. But he liked how the sea had rubbed away their edges, and he ran his hands over sections that were smooth.

It was noon, and he looked at the clock. This was typically the time for his walk, which he counted on. He had delivered mail for most of his working life, so he had spent much of it walking.

This is how he had met his wife. She was a seamstress. Thread, thimbles, needles, and bolts of silk and taffeta had to be delivered to her almost daily, and the frequency of that led to conversation. His dark eyes and measured restraint drew her to him, and she, too, was quiet yet pleasing, which appealed to him. She was kind with an old world sense of elegance, and though she was modest in dress, she had long lines, and she knew how to draw attention to that. Her speech he also found pleasing, and she sang occasionally, which he found bold in their small town. Having met late in life, they had no children, and desired none, but they both had an interest in civic matters and knew most everyone in the town that they lived.

In his case, he'd had an unexceptional life. An only child with older parents, he had always been introspective. Mail carrying seemed the ideal profession, his parents thought. "You'll get to know everyone in town," his parents said, "and you'll never have to go far." Later, he realized it was isolating; people always assumed he had important work or official business, which made them reluctant to start conversations, and because he tended to be shy, he rarely initiated speaking. Instead, he would tip

15

his hat, or nod, or make quick smiles or raises of the eyebrow to indicate "good morning," "goodbye," or an occasional, "nothing much I can do."

Their romance had an air of fate about it. Her house was filled with fabric wrapped around mannequins or bolts stacked neatly in alcoves. He would deliver stacks of boxes, multiple layers high, filled with spools of thread and ribbon or sometimes heavy bolts of fabric. She often asked him to stay as she opened them to check on the accuracy of her order. Soon he was accepting her offers of cookies, cakes, teas, and chocolates. He began to help her lift boxes or hold bolts as she measured them. Weekday visits turned into weekend events, and he started to escort her to the evening concerts in the park.

Their talk centered around work and her projects, and he admired her restraint. She seemed uninterested in gossip or what he might learn from delivering the mail. She thought of him as noble, someone entrusted with important, official work, and he carried it out in a trustworthy fashion. After a year, they felt deeply tied and they married. By then his parents had passed, as had hers, and the town surrounded them sweetly, pleased that two lonely birds had somehow found a way to each other.

They were happy and easily pleased by each other's company. He became melancholic only on occasion, and when she would inquire, he would say only that he had once aspired to be a part of something great or grand, to which she responded with a hand on his wrist, and closed eyes, saying, "You will."

When he and his wife had retired, they found little need to go anywhere new or to start anything ambitious. They often didn't say where or why when either of them went out. What she enjoyed in her home was ironing sheets, curtains, napkins, their clothes, and on occasion, wrinkled currency. It soothed her. As a seamstress she was known for the precision of her pleats, tucks, and delicate piping, which often required careful pressing. She liked the weight of the iron and the hiss of steam rising up to her face. It brought pink to her cheeks though her skin was already lovely.

Whatever they did in their free time kept them busy, and they didn't speak much. Whether they were quietly independent or increasingly aloof, others couldn't tell.

That morning, after sorting the seven pieces he had found, he felt something new as he stepped out of the door of his house. He couldn't put his finger on it. As he made his way to the café, his attention was drawn to letters and pieces of letters. He didn't know if they had always been there, or whether they had now begun to appear, peeping out of an overly full trashcan or sticking out of a rain gutter, or lying on the street like a forgotten hubcap. A wooden tile here, a metal punctuation mark lay there, a spray of prepositions ("in," "on," "out," "under") teetering on a trash can lid. All of this, he noted.

As his walk to the café continued, his jaw tightened. Additional short phrases and punctuation marks seemed to be clustering in the street and on the pavement, some like debris, and others like clannish collections like young in a den. As he walked, he wasn't sure of what he was seeing. *I don't think I've noticed this before,* he thought.

As he rounded the corner to the café, with his wooden cane on his arm and in his good woolen coat, he chose a table on the sidewalk, even though it was cold. He liked to watch the people, and he liked to see the warmth rise from his hot tea. Today, from his table, he watched a woman speak, and he thought he saw, as if in a cartoon dialogue bubble, lines and squiggles emerge from her lips instead of words as she spoke, and he mentally rearranged her conversation in his own thought bubble as she talked. Although he hadn't had such an experience before, he didn't think much about it, and he continued to sit, and later forgot about her as he drank his strong, dark tea.

He read his paper thoroughly and began to feel foolish. The letters on the printed paper sat obediently, and nothing in the headlines moved. It wasn't as if all words or letters had become animated. He laughed to himself, and when done with reading and people-watching, he began his walk home. However, as he did, he found himself side stepping increasing piles of letters, commas, semicolons, colons, question marks and even exuberant exclamation marks lying on the ground. As he walked, he looked around him to see if anyone else in the town was noticing. They didn't seem to. Everyone went about their business, sweeping letters as if they were leaves fallen from a tree, or walking around stacks of periods and commas, as if they were deliveries, waiting for someone to claim them. *Maybe this is how it has always been,* he thought.

When he got home, he saw a small stack in front of his door similar to what he had seen all morning. He tapped his newspaper several times on his other gloved hand, as if working through his mind what he might do. Then in a sudden move, he scooped up two stray wooden tiles (letters "B" and "Y") and a punctuation mark (a very worn, round period with hairline cracks) and carried them to his little woodshed on the side of the house.

Reaching into an old jar on a shelf above the doorway, he pulled out a key and unlocked the door. He paused again as if to think, but then gave an emphatic push to the creaking doors, suddenly letting light into the dank, spider-filled workshop.

The light from the door filled the room as if a globe of light had been placed in it, and with his gloved hands, he brushed off dust and old leaves from the worktable. He set down the odd pieces he had been carrying and walked out, re-locking the door behind him.

That night at dinner he was quiet with his wife, and she was too. The cat lay at the foot of the bed, purring loudly, and they were asleep by nine.

As the air became cooler and the moon rose, he slipped into a deep, deep sleep. He found himself in wild colorful dreams, full of flying inkwells, pens, sharpened pencils, quills, typewriter keys, and swimming seas full of vowels and consonants. He dreamt of letters. He saw punctuation marks popping up between the leaves of giant Savoy cabbages and vowels nestled in among the farmers' tidy rows of growing squash and potatoes. He saw red wheelbarrows full of harvested letters being pushed to farmers markets where kerchiefed women tied letters, phrases, and coordinators like "for," "and," "nor," "but," "or," "yet," and "so" into brown paper bundles and laid them in rows next to bouquets of flowers on their wooden tables.

The next morning, he woke late to find his wife had already left the house. He went straight away to the workshop. Once in the shed, he opened up an old cupboard, pulled out on an old workman's apron, visor, and gloves, put them on and began to work.

He began by cleaning up the old letters, rubbing the dirt off of them and hammering out dents in the metal punctuation marks. One mark took on a lovely sheen. Sitting with just "B" and "Y," he sat back looking at them. In a moment or two, he got up outside and chose an "S," "F," "H", "M," the "W" from the previous day and some vowels, some slightly chipped, from a neighbor's overflowing trash can. After rinsing and drying them, he started moving them around, into combinations and strings, playing with different configurations, adding letters, discarding others. Then finally, just as it was growing dark, he seemed satisfied.

He stood back and looked at his work.

Birds fly.
Fish swim.

"Ah, life is simple," he said. "A thing that is complete can stand alone."

"A sentence contains an actor—or an agent—" and he put a question mark, "*and* an action or state of being," which he carefully wrote in a notebook as he sat on his bench.

He clicked off the light, gave a quick cluck of satisfaction and went to bed. Again, that night he and his wife had a quiet dinner, but they were both in good spirits. They seemed eager for the peace of night and fell asleep holding hands, which they had not done in years.

The next day, when he went out for the morning paper, he found a package addressed in childlike writing to "Mr. M." He picked it up and looked to the right and left of him to see if anyone was watching. He stepped back into the house and opened it. He clipped off the string and took off the stiff brown paper that had wrapped a nearly new set of coordinating conjunctions. He touched the letters, which were set in a smooth ceramic white tile, and repeated the first letters of each word, "F," "A," "N," "B," "O," "Y," "S." The letters in blue on the white tiles were not unlike the blue willow china loved by his wife.

He had a quick breakfast of tea and oats and started his work in the shed. He walked to the to the back alley of the street and saw a small stack of nouns, some broken and others complete, next to a bin. A perfect complement for the set of unexpected conjunctions that had come to his door. "Magnificent seven," he thought.

His wife, home that day, chose to stitch little sacks, which she then ironed, to keep some of the chip-free letters he had found and polished. In the afternoon, two neighbors brought worn out words and letters along with steaming pots of food and pie. Through the window, as she ironed, his wife saw two teens sitting on a curb tossing abandoned letters "P" and "Q" back and forth, and a toddler sat in the park grass with a broken question mark in her hand. A child about seven, ran with a stick pushing the letter "O" down the road. Another child hooked the lowercase "g" upside down on a tree limb and swung on it like a swing.

That day he used all seven conjunctions he had received.

He stood back and looked at them beneath the lamplight of the shed.

"Life compounds," he thought. "One thing is connected to another," he said, raising his index finger to the sky for emphasis.

> They had chosen each other, **for** each was good and kind.

> He loved her, **and** she loved him.

> At times, he didn't understand her, **nor** did she understand him.

> They often struggled with this, **but** they chose not to express it.

> This made life difficult, **yet** they remained together.

> They believed in persevering , **so** they chose not to give up.

"There are ways to connect clauses that are independent and complete and to show relationships between them," he wrote.

Fatigued from the day, his wife had fallen asleep early, and he and the cat joined her, with the moon falling into the room from the window.

As they both slept, early that morning, news of his interest in words spread. Soon a faded red truck pulled up and unloaded a pile of words as high as a gravel pile might be for a driveway, and all of them were subordinators. The "when," "while," "if," "because," "until," "though," "even though," "although," unless" were mixed with noun clauses of "whatever you do," everything you say," and "wherever you go," with adverb clauses of "because it was right," "if they did this," next to adjective clauses of "who ran a mile," "that cared enough," and "who wore a string of pearls." These all sat outside their door as the sun rose.

Over breakfast he and his wife seemed unmoved by the unexpected bounty. Within the hour he began hammering and polishing what had arrived. Too, he welded back together broken punctuation marks that had been rummaged from scrap heaps on the previous day. The decorative storage sacks had also become larger to accommodate entire sentences intended to be given later as gifts.

This took him several days, and he had more time to mull over how he might arrange them. It was not easy attaching the dependent clauses to the independent clauses. He worked slowly and deliberately, taking breaks often and sleeping early at night. Then after finishing this all, he stepped back and looked.

After he studied the lines in careful rows, he wrote, "Life is complex. One thing is dependent on the other." He looked over what he had put together.

Everything she did made me happy.

They remembered *what was really important*.

She stayed *even though she sometimes wanted to go*.

If birds can fly, words can swim.

When he thought of her, she thought of him.

Wherever she'd go, he'd want to go.

Why it worked, he didn't know.

He changed *because he wanted to*.

"The dependent must rely on the independent; the dependent cannot stand alone," he penciled in his notes, with a strange thrill of emotion.

The next week, when both subordinators and coordinators came, delivered this time in the middle of the night into their small yard, it took him even longer to arrange them properly, but when he did, he asked his wife to look at them with him.

They stood back from them the next morning in the early light.

Why it worked, he didn't know; at times, he didn't understand her, **nor** did she understand him.

This made life difficult, **yet** they remained together; they remembered *what was really important.*

Everything she did made him happy, **so** *wherever she went*, he wanted to go.

If birds could fly and words could swim, he could love her **and** she could love him.

They looked at each other and saw the reflections of themselves in the polished exclamation marks lying on the floor.

That night he wrote on the last page of his notebook, "Life is compound-complex! We connect and depend on each other."

In the weeks that followed, the people in town mailed him letters and punctuation in small boxes. Mothers held the hands of their children and knocked on their door, carrying bits and pieces of used alphabet letters and other parts of speech. His wife also found a system to distribute sacks of new sentences by leaving them outside the door so people could pick them up on their way home. Once a week she held little refresher classes with a chalkboard, pointer, and notes from her husband. People in the town began to miss the past; they wanted to regain the way they used to arrange and rearrange letters and words. They started again: first in phrases, then sentences, then paragraphs.

As the months passed, her husband was able to cut back the time spent on the letters, and he began to take in only the words he truly felt an affinity for. He and his wife enjoyed spending more time together, marveling at the handiwork each could produce, and feeling humbled by the joy their gifts brought to the town, especially to the children. On some days, they found themselves taking a walk by the water, collecting an errant letter or two that floated up onto the sand, although finding those had become infrequent.

Gradually, the degree to which the floating thoughts, letters, and punctuation marks were abandoned began to decrease. There was little excess or discarding of pieces. The children sat in school polishing letters and gave them as gifts to their parents. The elderly began to remember the previous years of tender language and earnest sentences.

Mr. M would reflect upon this whenever he found that the now rare, stray comma that might be in search of a place in the world. He would tuck it carefully under his arm and bring it home, looking forward to rendering it new again. For, despite having done this many times, and though he did this much now more judiciously, he did so gratefully. And so did his wife, who looked at him with such fullness at times, their both having found so late in life such grand purpose in love, words, and this new but changing peace.

The End

Acknowledgments

Many thanks to my family and friends who have encouraged my love of words. Much appreciation also to Bobbie Felix, who helped me understand both language and friendship. And thank you also to my students, who made me try harder to be a better teacher and writer. I'll always be learning, and I don't think that will ever change.

Author's Note

Language is always shifting and reinventing itself. How we use it and how we perceive it also changes. Although there are "rules," and Mr. M in *Floating* plays with those, these rules and their applications are highly dependent on the situation, the mode of communication, the language of the individuals and groups we're communicating with, and their style choices. It's also affected by the purpose we have at that moment. Mr. M's use of words and his decisions about sentences are based on his world and his context. And although he is drawn by the shape of words initially, something beneath that drives him. What I take from Rumi is this: If we tend to the deeper aspects, to the "inner bond" with each other that he speaks of, we'll find the truth of things eventually, beyond the shape of words.

About the Author

Pianta is a poet, fiction writer, and editor, whose work has appeared in journals such as *Nimrod International Journal*, *Adirondack Review*, *Ekphrasis*, *Terrain.org*, and *Bamboo Ridge Press*, among others. Her readings often incorporate live music and other media. Her projects include a novella, *Old Volcano Road* and a CD, *Little Bird: Songs for Children*. Her website can be found at www.pianta.org.

Resources

Purdue University Owl Writing Resources
https://owl.purdue.edu/

Guide to Grammar and Writing
Sponsored by Capital Community College Foundation
http://guidetogrammar.org/grammar/

For multilingual learners and teachers
The English Page
https://www.englishpage.com/

Traditional style guide
The Chicago Manual of Style
https://www.chicagomanualofstyle.org/home.html

For a resource on gender, race, and issues of inclusivity
related to language
The Conscious Style Guide
https://consciousstyleguide.com/

For those interested in language and second language
studies
University of Hawai'i Second Language Studies Program
https://www.hawaii.edu/sls/

Illustration Credits

Photo of man with umbrella, iStock shots; Ocean waves, Issara, iStock; Background fish scene ai-generated by Bianca van Dijk, Pixabay.

Releases

Old Volcano Road
Novella
Ebook and print versions
Available on Kindle and Amazon

Little Bird: Songs for Children
CD of original acoustic children's songs
Available on iTunes and Apple Music
Listen to samples at
https://pianta.hearnow.com/

Short Fiction

Floating
Ebook on Apple Books
Amazon.com

Poetry

Hawai'i Poems: from there to here
Book of new and previously published poems
Amazon.com

We Don't Know What We Don't Know
Poetry Chapbook
Amazon.com

All Ends Never End
Poetry Chapbook
Amazon.com

Before
Poetry Chapbook
Amazon.com

A Man in Parts
Poetry Chapbook
Amazon.com

Acts and Intentions
Poetry Chapbook
Amazon.com

Love and Grief in the Time of Ketu
Poetry chapbook
Amazon.com

For more information
www.pianta.org